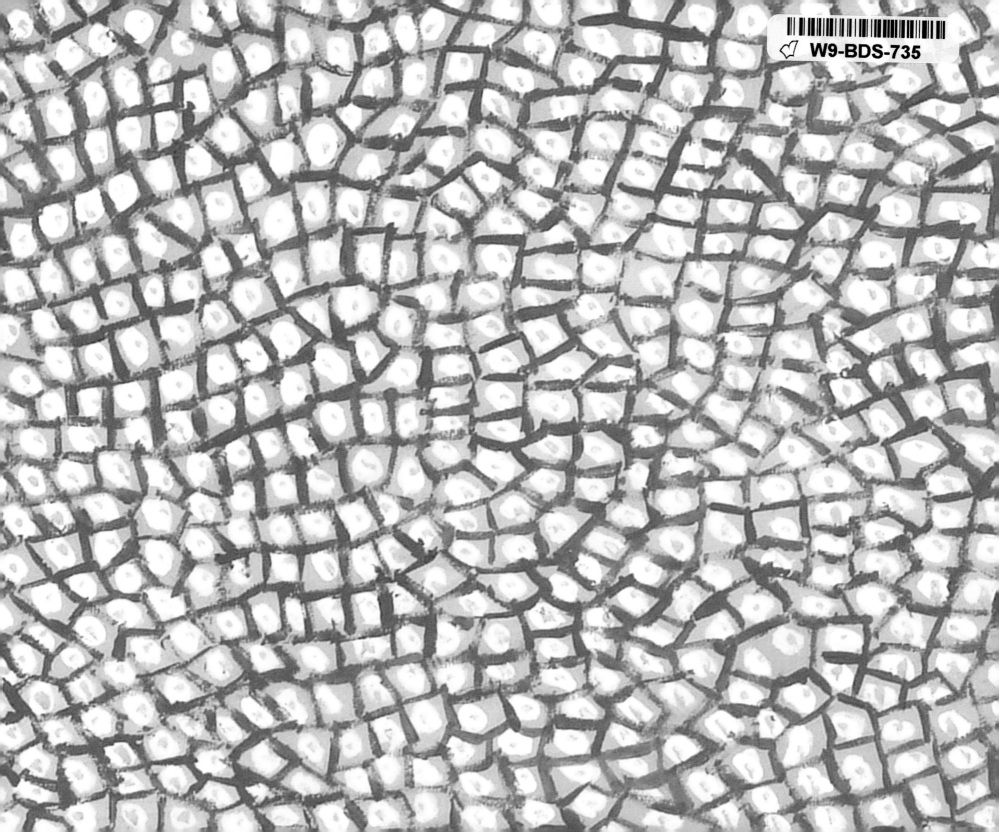

This Book Belongs To Me

Inside Outside Who We Are

Written by **Steve Tiller**   Accompanied by the art of **Harry Teague**

MichaelsMind

Steve Tiller, Author
Harry Teague, Artist
Robert Cremeans, Creative Director / Art Director
Kathryn L. Tecosky, Editor
Victoria DeLoach, Photographer

Special thanks to: Our Families, CCAD, David & Melissa Abbey, Alana Shepherd, Mike and Shannon Francklin,
Barbara and Barry Klein, Terri Potter, Ben Tiller PC tech wiz, Alan Carter, Mary Zeman, Brian Bias our Apple
guru, Scott Stettler at Brand EXX.

Library of Congress Cataloging-in-Publication Data
Tiller, Steve

Summary:
A book that allows us to celebrate the differences that make each of us unique and special.

ISBN 1-932317-08-2
[1. Multiculturalism - Children's Fiction.   2. Diversity - Fiction.   3. Interfaith -Self Esteem

Printed by
Regal Printing Hong Kong

Harry Teague's Paintings were created with acrylic paint on mat board

Visit us for fun and games at:
www.michaelsmind.com

Or visit Harry and Diannia at:
www.harryteague.com

To our family and friends with a special thanks
to Charlene Ediger who helped take Harry's
boredom into a new direction with lots of color!

-Harry and Diannia Teague

Dedicated to Shannon, Mike, and Kira Francklin.
Three stories written by Life's Author full of
miracles, courage, hope, and tenacity. I am proud
to call you my friends.

-ST

When I look at you
It isn't hard to see,
You really do not look
Very much like me!

I'm a boy
You're a girl,
I have straight hair
You have curls.

You have big hands
Mine are small,
Your arms are long
My legs are tall.

Look At Us 2004

We don't match
In how we look,
So, should the cover
Judge the book?

You are yellow
I am white,
You have dark eyes
Mine are light.

I like long hair
Yours is short.
My toes are stubby,
"Hey, there's a wart!"

Footies 2004

I am black
You are round,
I am thin
You are brown.

I wear glasses
You wear hats,
Your feet are big
My nose is flat.

Nobody is the same,
You know!
We're all different
As we grow!

Unique Pair 2004

Some are deaf,
Some can't talk.
Some are blind,
Some can't walk.

Forget the looks,
Inside's the same!
Just say "Hello!
What's your name?"

They may not be
The same as you,
But they all love
To make friends too!

We Are Together 2004

Different looks
Lots of faces!
Different names
From lots of places!

You are Rachel,
I am Marcy.
There's Janet, Ben,
Dylan, Darcy.

Here's Mike, Kira,
Shannon, Bob,
Alina, Blue,
Noah, Rob!

Away We Slide 2004

Alex, Hayden,
Kenzie, Larry,
Brooke, Boosie,
Katie, Harry.

Maddie, Missy,
Sara, Sam,
Ali, Chin
Lee and Pam.

Lots of people
Different races,
Here together
Sharing spaces!

Holding the String 2004

What we think
Is not alike,
We all find things
That we dislike.

I eat hot dogs,
Don't like greens.
You eat veggies,
Don't like beans.

You wear jeans
Don't like skirts,
I wear blouses
Don't like shirts.

Two Toasting 2004

We don't have to
Think the same.
Doesn't matter,
There's no blame!

You love birds
I like dogs,
I ride horses
You kiss frogs!

I milk cows
You love bats,
I like fish
And lazy cats!

Fearrington Village 2004

We disagree
On lots of stuff,
But how we feel
Is close enough.

We think different
In our mind,
But our feelings
Are the same we find.

Inside our hearts
We all feel love,
For friends and family
And things above!

Downtown 2004

Our words describe
What we see,
But you can't see
Inside of me!

Clowning faces
Funny hats,
We all can laugh
At stuff like that!

Some are old
Some are young,
But Purple Pops
Get purple tongues.

Just The Four Of Us 2004

We all like fun
And getting hugs,
But please, no spiders
Or squishy slugs!

We love swings
With windy hair,
And guessing cloud
Shapes in the air.

We love exploring
Lots of things,
Like smelling flowers
In the Spring.

Swimg Set Fun 2004

We all have trust
And plans that fly,
Like soaring kites
In bright blue skies.

We all love
Crunching candy,
Taking dares,
Tying ribbons in our hair!

We are the same
In many things,
We love to joke
We love to sing.

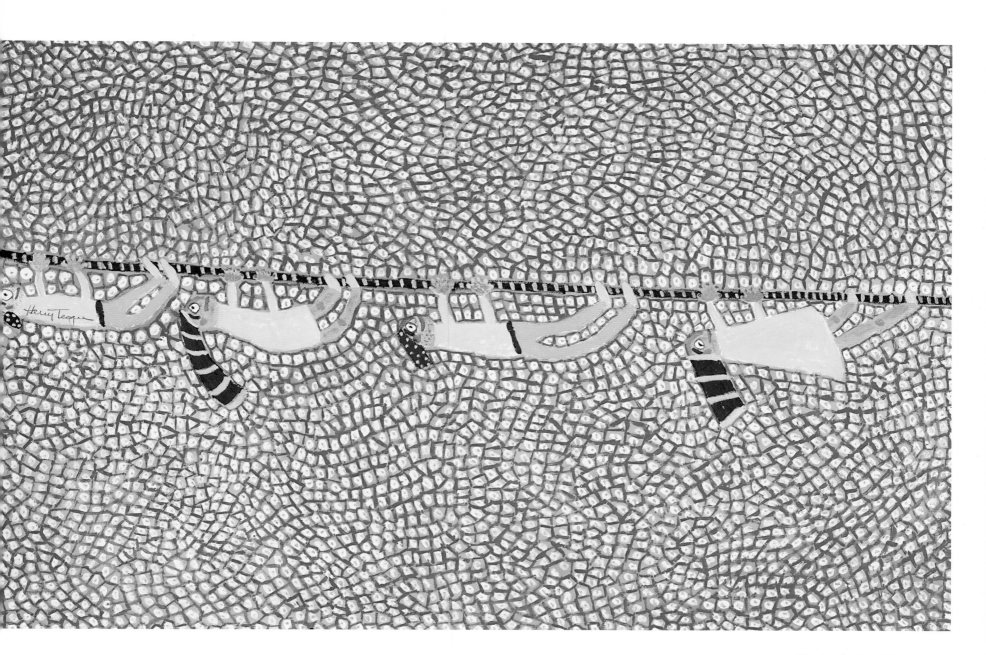

Hanging On Line 2004

Teachers tell us
Just be kind.
Pledge the Flag,
Stand in line.

Be polite and
Wait your turn,
Avoid hot stoves
They can burn.

Look both ways
Crossing steets,
Wash your hands
Wipe your feet!

American Flag 2004

When I use
My heart to see,
I find you feel
The same as me!

Some would like
To be a Star!
Or be accepted
For who they are.

We all just want
To get along,
And really feel
Like we belong!

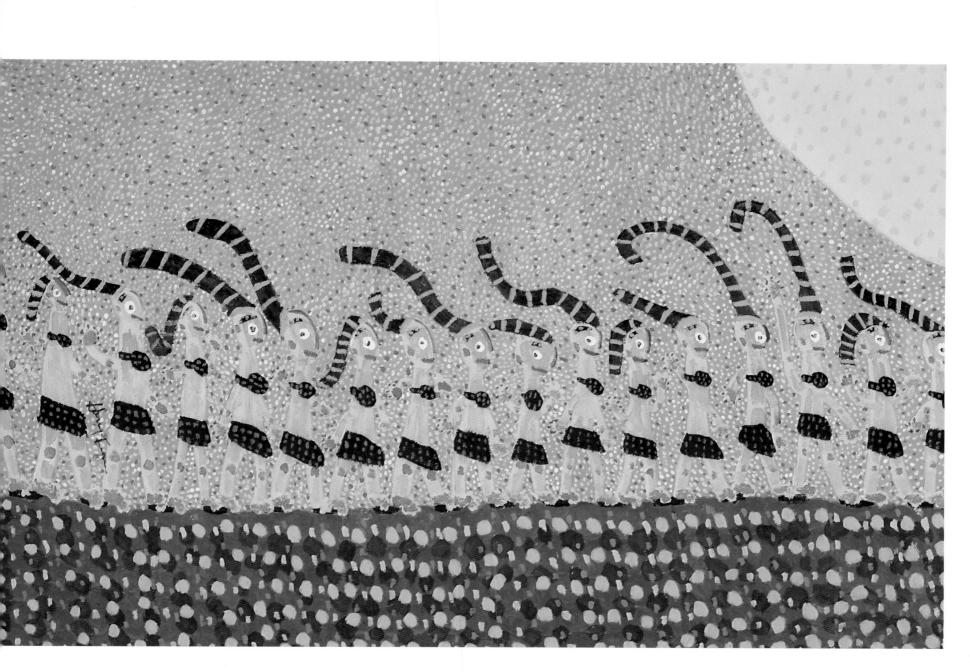

I Volunteer 2004

We're not so different
As it seems,
In our hopes
And in our dreams!

We all want love,
We all have fears.
We all love laughter,
We all cry tears.

I am really
Just like you!
And in your heart
You know it's true!

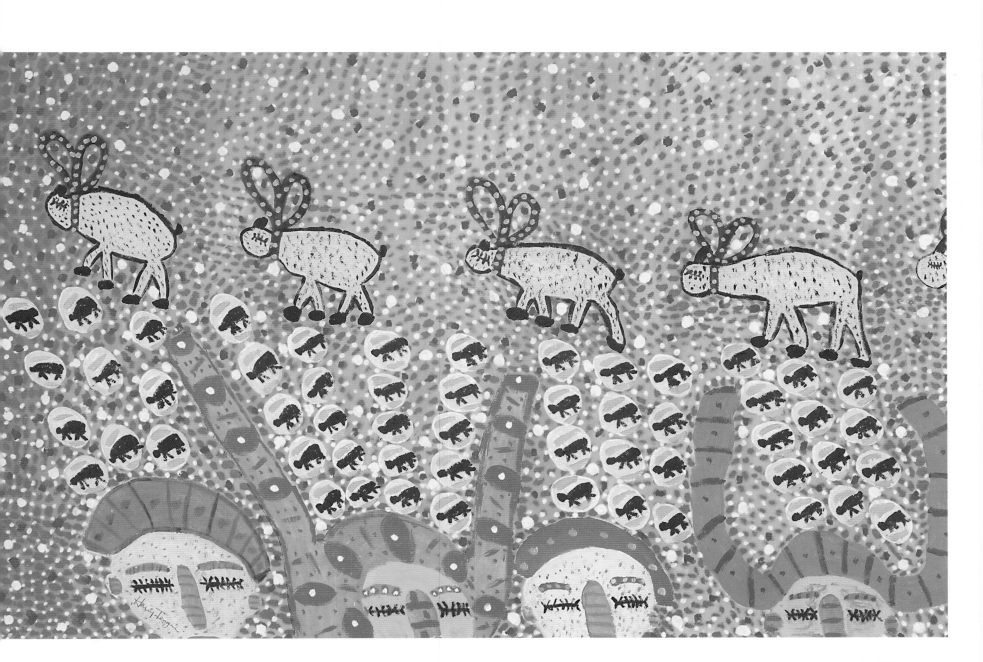

Nite Nite 2004

The Spirit behind
Our living tree
Makes us family,
Can't you see?

Like birds that fly
We live together,
Different birds
Different feathers.

You and me
Part of a plan,
The great and growing
Clan of Man!

One Hundred and Twenty Toes 2004

The En d

Harry and Diannia Teague's world changed forever in 1990 when Harry survived a stroke. Harry's art therapy tapped into a new creative ability for expression and communication. Their efforts in art together have brought them new adventures and friends. To know them is to marvel at the adaptability of the human spirit. Each painting we see, and each meeting with these partners in art and life, is a reminder to the rest of us that when one door closes another door opens. It is with much pleasure that Harry and Diannia share with us Harry's colorful voice of art.

I have always had outdoor animals. I do better inside. I have allergies. I figure the animals do better outside. If they need to go, they are already in the right place. They can just go.

I don't win many arguments around my house. My son has three cats. All the cats are female All live inside.

The girls had a black lab. Female, of course. Another inside animal. That dog cost a lot of money. Don't know why. It wasn't very smart. That dog had less a sense of smell than I do. It would get to the end of the driveway, look confused, and just wander off.

After a few days someone would call telling us they had the dog. We'd go get it. It would find the end of the driveway again, then couldn't figure out how to turn around and come back up the driveway. After about the 400th phone call to come get the dog, I had the number changed, but by then it was too late. Everyone knew where we lived.

My daughters wanted a cat.. They got a stray that had been "fixed". That cat turned out to be crazy. It would roam around the house at night screaming in the dark. It would never let anybody touch it. Kind of looked like that Bill the Cat character. I thought she had a good appetite. She kept getting fatter and fatter. We finally figured out that the cat had not been fixed.

She had four kittens. Of course, we had to keep at least one of those. It is an indoor animal. After the mother had kittens. She disappeared. I must admit I didn't run out to look for her.

The kitten opens the kitchen cabinets doors and sleeps in a drawer. It is pretty scary when something jumps out at you when you are sneaking around in the dark trying to get a late night snack. We have a bunny named Bubbles. It is female too. You guessed it. The rabbit lives inside too. Something about the hawks. I sometimes wonder how rabbits have survived all these eons.

I finally had some decent luck with an animal. A dog wondered up one day. It was skittish. It wouldn't get too close at first. This dog almost makes you laugh to look at him. He looks like the left over parts of other dogs. Big head, long body and short legs. It is a Shepett. Part Basset Hound and part German Shepherd. Great dog. Real smart. We named him FrankenDog, but mostly call him Buddy. I thought there is no way this dog will ever want to come into the house. I went out of town for a couple days and by the time I got back my wife had that dog sleeping on the couch. Now, it barks at me whenever I come up to the house. At least, it is a male.

Now that summer has come, I wonder if my allergies would do better if I lived outside.

Steve Tiller   2006

Award Winning Books by MichaelsMind

Call your favorite bookstore and give them our phone number - or you can order from us directly if you want your books autographed or personalized for gifts.

Tangle Fairies $15.95

"It's a funny little story- I am sure you've never heard. You may think it's kind of silly, probably absurd. Why- no matter if you comb your hair before you go to bed, in the morning when you wake up, you got tangles in your head!"
Reviewers said "Tangle Fairies is one of those books the kids will want to read again and again. The tiny fairies with iridescent wings and rainbow colored hair are just like children would imagine them to be."
Benjamin Franklin Award

Connected at the Heart $15.95

My daughter, Rachel, wanted a birthday story- so I put her up in Heaven waiting to be born. Rachel began to think she was going to get lost or be late until she discovers that she is connected to the heart of her mother- and she could never possibly get lost!
Reviewers called it "poignant and heartwarming and suitable for personal libraries, schools and Sunday School libraries." It is a great gift for a new mom especially if there is an older child in the home, or as a gift for Mother's Day!
Writer's Digest Merit Recommendation

Henry Hump Born to Fly $15.95

Henry is a caterpillar who is suspicious of cocoons, and isn't very eager to visit one real soon! But he soon learns that if we take time to look carefully beneath the leaf – we can discover hope and optimism even in the face of overwhelming change!
Reviewers said "Tiller's strength is his lighthearted approach to deep spiritual questions…Cremeans's technicolor illustrations make each bug bigger than life!"
Visionary Award

Just Be Yourself! $15.95

Let your individuality shine through in everything you do! Feel good about who you are! We are all unique with different strengths and talents. The world needs those differences expressed wisely and usefully. "There is just one on the planet exactly like you! There won't be another there can never be two! Be bold and be brave, always give your best try. Life has no limits, so keep aiming high!"
NEW for 2006

Boat & Wind $15.95

A simple conversation between a little boat and the wind about belief in things that can't be seen, Boat & Wind highlights the importance of faith and friendship in our daily lives. Reviewers said "The beautiful illustrations evoke the feeling of being at sea. Pages beam with texture and depth. The story is strong and the message important." Another reviewer said it "portrays the deep meaning of faith with childlike simplicity and unique clarity.
Georgia Author of the Year for Children's Literature

Rainbow's Landing $15.95

This book is a beautifully illustrated underwater adventure about having the courage to follow our dreams Fred the sea anemone learns the dreams we hold in our hearts can guides to finding our purpose in life. The book has a great message and vibrant, techicolor illustrations!
Reviewers said Rainbow's Landing "presents a valuable lesson with playful compassion. The illustrations keep you looking for new details hidden in the glow of the sea."
Georgia Author of Year Finalist

Santa's Red Nose Rocket $15.95

Pinky, the space alien, crash lands at the North Pole. She asks Santa about the meaning of Christmas. Santa tells the real Christmas story! "Elves dressed as kings brought him gifts from afar…" Pinky heads back to the stars spreading the message of love and hope!
The best review is from people who call me for more personalized copies for the children of friends and relatives as gifts. This is a very unique and wonderful Christmas story.
Georgia Author of the Year Finalist

Inside Outside Who We Are $15.95

Diversity makes life interesting. Individual differences can also be the source of problems between people. When we look at others with our eyes -everybody is always different from ourselves. But if we close our eyes for a moment, and look with our heart instead of our mind- it turns out that everyone is really very much the same! "We are not so different as it seems. We all have hopes, we all have dreams! In your heart, you know it's true! I am very much like you!"
NEW for 2006

All of MichaelsMind books are fun. All have great illustrations. All carry a positive message. All openly discuss common values of American life such as courage, love, faith, hope, family, tolerance, and individuality. Public and Private schools use our books in value and character education programs.

Books can be ordered at our website **www.michaelsmind.com** by email **satiller@juno.com** or calling **404-314-1348** or **Fax 404-531-0360**. Payments may be made by check or credit card. Let us know if you want the books autographed or personalized as gifts. We support schools, literacy efforts and children's hospitals. Our books are often used as fundraisers.

"Thanks for your support!"